To .... James "2018" ....

For being good.
MERRY
CHRISTMAS!
From Santa

Santa's Sleigh

is on its way to

Hawaii

To my family ... the best present ever x

Visit the author's website! http://ericjames.co.uk

Written by Eric James
Illustrated by Robert Dunn and Amerigo Pinelli
Designed by Sarah Allen

Published by Sourcebooks Jabberwocky, an imprint of Sourcebooks, Inc.
P.O. Box 4410, Naperville, Illinois 60567-4410
(630) 961-3900
Fax: (630) 961-2168
jabberwockykids.com

Date of Production: June 2017
Run Number: HTW_PO100417
Printed and bound in China (GD)
10 9 8 7 6 5 4 3 2

Santa's Sleigh
is on its way to
Hawaii

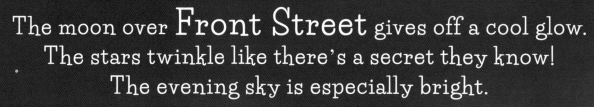

The moon over Front Street gives off a cool glow.
The stars twinkle like there's a secret they know!
The evening sky is especially bright.

"Hey Santa! Hey Santa!
Please visit tonight!"

The wind-chimes in Pearl City swing in the breeze.
The North Wind blows through Honolulu's palm trees.

In Hana sweet carols are heard on the air.
The magic of Christmas is felt everywhere!

The Christmas trees twinkle,
The eggnog smells sweet,
The stockings are out
(for the gifts, not your feet!)

The garlands and
paper-chains
hang from
the ceiling,
And give the
whole household
that Christmassy
feeling.

Excited young children
with heads full of wishes
Leave large Christmas cookies
and carrots on dishes.

They scurry upstairs,
for they've heard
it is said
That Santa comes
once you're asleep
in your bed!

In Kaneohe the yawns become stronger and stronger.
The children of Laie can't stay up much longer.
From Ewa to Kula, and Waimea too,
They're soon sleeping soundly,

All children but you!

You stand at your window
and gaze at the sky,
With hopes that you'll see
Santa's sleigh *whizzing* by.
You almost nod off,
but see movement ahead...

...A flurry of white and some flashes of red!

You jump up and down as the shape becomes clear.
"Hey Santa! Hey Santa!
My home's over here!"

But something is wrong. There are sparks EVERYWHERE.
The sleigh *twists* and *turns* as it swoops through the air.

You're wide awake now.
You've had such a fright.
There's no chance of sleep
till you know he's alright.

You think about Santa,
his reindeer and sleigh.
"Hey Santa!
Hey Santa!
I hope you're okay!"

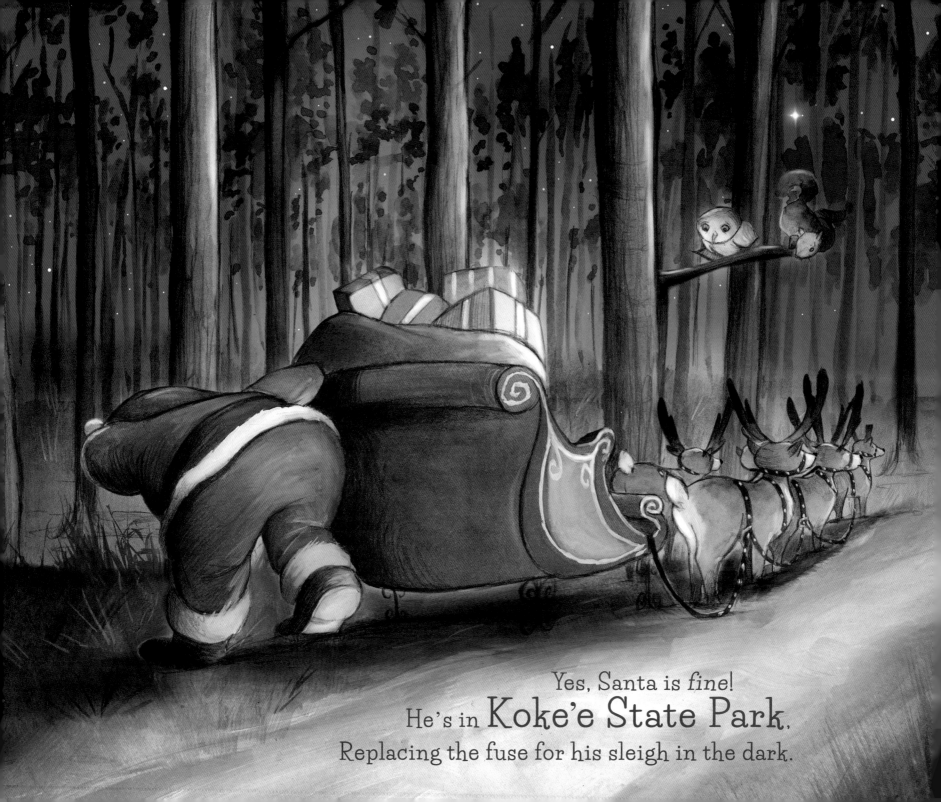

Yes, Santa is fine!
He's in Koke'e State Park,
Replacing the fuse for his sleigh in the dark.

He tugs on the reins, shouting,
"UP, UP, AWAY!"
And hits the ignition,
which starts up his sleigh.

KOKE'E
STATE
PARK

With magical speed only Santa possesses, he visits well over a thousand addresses.

From Hilo to Kapaa,
delivering toys,
He visits each house
without making a noise.

Now Santa has been to all houses but one.
He can't go back home till this last house is done.

It's YOUR house, of course, but you're still wide awake.
He circles above as he takes a small break.
And that's when you see him. You know he's alright!
Your head hits the pillow. You're out like a light.

He lands on the roof to the sound of your snores.
"It's Santa! It's Santa!
He's coming indoors!"

But, ARGH!

You wake up and you jump to your feet.

You're sure you forgot to leave Santa a treat.

Will Santa leave presents for someone so rude?!

You must go downstairs

and make sure he has food!

You enter the kitchen
and turn on the light,
Not spotting the figure
who ducks out of sight.

You're still half-asleep,
so you don't find it weird
That the broom has a hat
...and a coat
...and a beard!

You get out the cookies, still rubbing your eyes,
Too blurry to make out his clever disguise.
You open the fridge door,

but don't spot the **broom**
As it sweeps past you into...

...the family room!

With a plate in your hands, you head off to the tree.
You're feeling so sleepy you don't even see
A sight that would have your heart
skipping a beat—
The curtains have sprouted...

...two Santa-sized feet!

Still sleepy, you head back
to bed with a smile.
The panic is over.
It's all been worthwhile.

You climb up the staircase,
not once looking back,
As a chuckling Santa
takes toys from his sack.

Ho,
ho,
ho

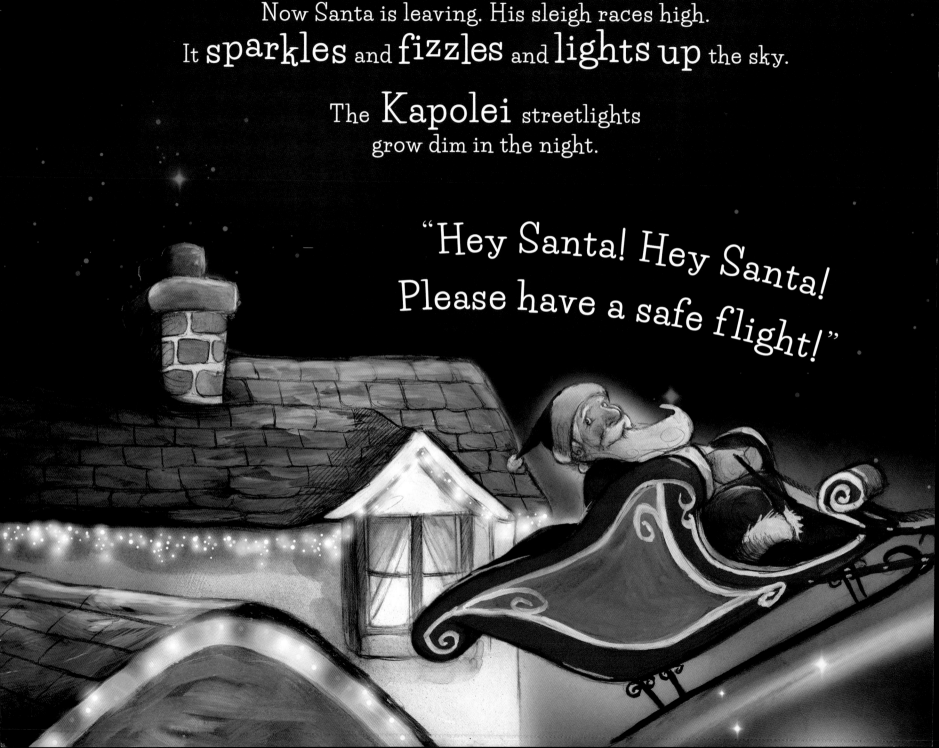

Now Santa is leaving. His sleigh races high.
It sparkles and fizzles and lights up the sky.

The Kapolei streetlights
grow dim in the night.

"Hey Santa! Hey Santa!
Please have a safe flight!"

Soon Santa leaves charming Hawaii behind,
Where children are lovely, and grown-ups are kind.
And then he **booms loudly,**
his voice full of cheer...

"Ho, ho, ho! **Hawaii**, I'll see you next year!"